Almost
Katharine the Great

The Red, White, and Blue Crew

by Lisa Mullarkey
illustrated by Phyllis Harris

magic wagon

visit us at www.abdopublishing.com

To Barbara Ammer: You get my vote!—LM

To my sisters, Pam and Patty:
Thanks for all your love and support. —PH

Published by Magic Wagon, a division of the ABDO Group, 8000 West 78th Street, Edina, Minnesota 55439. Copyright © 2009 by Abdo Consulting Group, Inc. International copyrights reserved in all countries. All rights reserved. No part of this book may be reproduced in any form without written permission from the publisher.

Calico Chapter Books™ is a trademark and logo of Magic Wagon.

Printed in the United States.

Text by Lisa Mullarkey
Illustrations by Phyllis Harris
Edited by Stephanie Hedlund and Rochelle Baltzer
Interior layout and design by Jaime Martens
Cover design by Jaime Martens

Library of Congress Cataloging-in-Publication Data

Mullarkey, Lisa.
  The Red, White, and Blue Crew / by Lisa Mullarkey ; illustrated by Phyllis Harris.
      p. cm. -- (Katharine the almost great ; bk. 5)
   ISBN 978-1-60270-583-8
   [1. Politics, Practical--Fiction. 2. Schools--Fiction.] I. Harris, Phyllis, 1962- ill. II. Title.
 PZ7.M91148Red 2009
 [E]--dc22
                                             2008036092

❀ CONTENTS ❀

❀ CHAPTER 1 ❀

Explode-a-Rama Election Drama

When the Statue of Liberty strolled into our classroom, I knew it would be a star-spangled day. Even with gobs of green face paint, a shiny crown, and bed sheets draped around her, I could still spot our principal.

"Hi, Mrs. Ammer."

She raised her torch. "Who's Mrs. Ammer? Call me Lady Liberty."

Mrs. Bingsley rushed over and shook her hand. "Welcome to our classroom!"

"I understand you're learning about democracy," said Lady Liberty as she bowed. "May I ask, what's a democracy?"

Vanessa Garfinkle stuck her hand up so high, she looked like a Statue of Liberty copycat. "A democracy is a government *of* the people, *by* the people, and *for* the people. Everyone works together to run the country and has the right to vote to help make decisions."

"Impressive, Vanessa!" said Lady Liberty, beaming. Her smile glowed as bright as the orange tissue paper stuffed inside her torch.

I glanced at my cousin Crockett and rolled my eyes. Leave it to Vanessa, aka Miss Priss-A-Poo, to memorize the Abraham Lincoln video we watched yesterday.

Lady Liberty straightened her crown. "Did you know the fourth and fifth graders hold elections every year to help make decisions in our school?"

"Don't *you* . . . ," I corrected myself. "I mean, I thought *Mrs. Ammer* made all the decisions." I waited for her to call me "impressive" since everyone knew that Ammer the Hammer was the head honcho at Liberty Corner School.

"Nope," said Lady Liberty. "If she did, I doubt she'd sit in the dunk tank on Fun Day each year."

Fun Day was revenge day! Kids waited all year for a chance to dunk Mrs. Ammer.

"I think it's time third graders helped with some decisions. So, we're going to hold an election," said Lady Liberty. "Is anyone interested in running for president?"

Hands shot into the air like geysers at Yellowstone National Park.

Mrs. Bingsley tapped her fingers on a poster of George Washington. "Your president must be an outstanding citizen."

I raised my hand. "Don't you think *I'd* make a super-duper president? Since my mom works here, I . . ."

Lady Liberty frowned. "It doesn't matter what *I* think. Your classmates vote."

My stomach did a flip-flop belly drop. "Did you know that the Baby Ruth candy bar was named after President Cleveland's daughter? It wasn't named after the baseball player." My calendar with 365 useless facts never lets me down!

Lady Liberty nodded. Then she wrote *responsible, honest,* and *fair* on the board. She circled responsible. "Being president is hard work and a huge responsibility. Your meetings are during recess."

Responsible was practically my middle name! Didn't I make my bed every morning? Well, except for today. And yesterday. And maybe a few days last week . . .

Lady Liberty traced over the words honest and fair. "These are important character traits that a president must have."

Before I declared myself a fair and square kind of girl, Vanessa leaned over and growled, "Remember kindergarten?"

How could I forget? Her mother wrote notes to her each day on her lunch napkins. But since Vanessa couldn't read, she'd ask me to read them to her. Before I did, I presto changed them a teensy-weensy bit.

Once her napkin said: *Have fun at your Halloween party.*

But I told her it said: *Give Katharine your chocolate candy.* She did!

My itty-bitty lies got me into mucho mega trouble. But I'm much older now.

I scribbled *fair* on a page in my math binder and felt sparkly because I'm a fair and square kid now. Most of the time. So maybe I don't always cut the last piece of cake into equal pieces to share with Crockett. If he didn't complain, it wasn't *unfair*, was it?

"Finally," said Lady Liberty, "you must have a platform. Ideas."

Bingo! I had oodles of ideas! Who thought of the Penny Harvest? Who thought of the recipe contest and cookbook? Who thought of drawing tattoos and Rent-a-Kid? Me! That's who!

She didn't say everyone had to like your ideas.

"Of course, your classmates will decide who's the most responsible, honest, and fair. They'll nominate the best candidates," said Mrs. Bingsley. "Look around and decide who has these characteristics."

Johnny waved to get my attention and gave me two thumbs-up.

Was he going to nominate me? I whipped my head around to look at Crockett, who was giving Johnny two thumbs-up. Maybe they were both nominating me!

I pulled my Luscious Lemon Lip Gloss out of my pocket and slathered it on. As president, I'd have to look my best at all times.

"Next week, you'll discuss platforms, give speeches, and vote," said Lady Liberty. "I think we're ready for nominations."

Rebecca raised her hand. "I nominate Vanessa."

Matthew shouted. "I nominate Johnny."

"And miss recess?" said Johnny. "No thanks!"

"Anyone else?" asked Lady Liberty.

I tapped my foot on the floor. What was taking Johnny and Crockett so long? Finally, Johnny spoke up. "I nominate the coolest kid in class . . ."

I licked my lips and shot out of my chair like a firecracker on the fourth of July.

This is what I thought he'd say:

"Katharine Carmichael."

But this is what he really said:

"Crockett!"

Crockett? What about me?

My per-fect-o star-spangled day turned into explode-a-rama election drama.

Why?

Because no one nominated me.

❀ **CHAPTER 2** ❀

The Magic Eight Ball Speaks

Miss Priss-A-Poo couldn't wait to brag about her nomination.

"Too bad you weren't nominated, Katharine." She waved a napkin in the air. "Maybe next year."

I twisted my pigtails. "I didn't want to run. Besides, Crockett will make a fab-u-lo-so president." I erased my math problem and blew rubber dust into the air. "His platform is top secret. You'll have to hear it to believe it."

I couldn't wait to find out myself.

❀ ❀ ❀

"I've got nothing," said Crockett as we walked home. "No platform. No ideas."

"Don't worry." I kicked a rock into the gutter. "I have bajillions!" I fired off so many, I felt dizzy. "Get rid of homework. Make every day pizza day! Let kids teach on Tuesdays. No school on Fridays." I saved the best for last. "Rip up math books!"

Crockett laughed. "Mrs. Ammer said we can't make promises we can't keep."

"Say it anyway," I said. "You'll get votes."

"That wouldn't be honest," said Crockett. "Or fair."

Maybe I wasn't as honest or fair as I thought. Maybe that's why my parents called me Katharine the *Almost* Great. They say I'm a work-in-progress. Maybe if I tried harder to be a little bit fairer and a lot more honest, they'd call me Katharine the Great. Then, maybe someone would nominate me for president next year.

During dinner, everyone fussed over Crockett. Even Jack!

Aunt Chrissy asked Jack, "Will Crockett lose the election?" Jack clapped and said, "No."

Dad asked, "Will Vanessa win the election?"

Jack said *no* again.

They passed Jack around like he was a Magic Eight Ball that could predict the future.

"Will Vanessa have a better platform than Crockett?" asked Aunt Chrissy.

"No," said Jack.

"Will Vanessa beat Crockett?" asked Mom.

"No," said Jack. Everyone laughed.

Since *no* was the only word Jack could say, I wasn't too impressed. By dessert, I was ready to ditch the whole conversation.

"Look, Crockett!" I swiped a Penelope Parks video off of the chair and waved it in the air. "I'll make the popcorn." We never missed our Friday movie nights.

Crockett shook his head. "Sorry. I need to work on my platform after I take out the recycling."

He knelt in the corner of the kitchen next to the bins he'd made in Junior Rangers. He plucked three *Teen Times* magazines out of the bin marked *newspapers* and sighed. "Do these look like newspapers?"

Ever since Crockett earned his Wilderness Survival Badge in Junior Rangers, he changed his name from William to Crockett. He said William was boring. And since he was a lot like Davy Crockett, King of the Wild Frontier, he wanted to be called Crockett.

He also started calling himself an "environmental warrior" and examined our toilet paper to make sure it was earth-friendly. Who knew unfriendly toilet paper existed?

If he wasn't saving the rain forest by using his allowance to buy acres, he was trying to figure out why honeybees were disappearing. He even made my mom switch to cloth napkins. And, he built different types of compost bins in the yard with my dad.

Crockett wasn't the type of kid to get mad easily. But if you messed with his bins, he'd get grumpier than Ammer the Hammer after her first dunk-a-roo in the tank.

"If we don't take better care of the planet," said Crockett, "it won't take care of us."

"Planet shmanet," I said. It's not that I didn't care about our planet but would it hurt to watch the Penelope Parks movie first? I dangled the video in front of his face. "How about we watch half?"

He grunted. "Vanessa probably has posters plastered in the hallways by now." He grabbed some twine, bundled the newspapers, and trudged downstairs.

I marched into the living room and ploppity plopped on the sofa.

"Why so glum, chum?" asked Dad.

I put my head in my mom's lap and felt comfy cozy as she stroked my hair. Her shirt smelled like the cinnamon puff cookies she'd baked at school. "Miss Priss-A-Poo was nominated and I wasn't."

Aunt Chrissy came out of the kitchen drying a pot. "Crockett wanted to nominate you, but when he heard about the speech, he was worried that you might . . . well . . . you know."

I lifted my head. "Barf again?"

My track record of having major barf-a-rama drama in front of crowds was legendary.

She nodded.

I bit my lip. How could everyone forget my per-fect-o performance in *Kids Rock in Space* already? "Did you know that cinnamon comes from the bark of a tree?"

Dad gave Mom the she's-trying-to-change-the-subject-again look. He kissed my forehead. "Crockett can't win without help," said Dad. "He needs a campaign manager."

"What's that?" I asked.

"A campaign manager is a person with great ideas who can get a crew of workers to make posters and convince others to vote for their candidate," Dad said. "I know the perfect person for the job."

"Who?" I asked.

"YOU!" shouted Mom, Dad, and Aunt Chrissy.

That's when I got an idea. A better-than-running-for-president idea.

I hopped off the couch and almost knocked over Jack, who had just pulled himself up by the coffee table. "Can I invite a few kids over to help with the election?"

"Sure," said Dad. "That's a great idea."

I raced to the phone and made three calls. Within 20 minutes, Tamara, Johnny, and Matthew were huddled on my front porch.

We tiptoed into the kitchen. Then, I jumped three times in front of the sink. That was my signal to Crockett that I needed him quicky quick!

Crockett flew up the stairs. "What are you guys doing here?"

I patted him on the back. "You're looking at your new campaign manager! And here," I said, pointing to everyone, "is your Red, White, and Blue Crew! We're going to get you elected, Mr. President."

"I hope so," said Crockett shifting from foot to foot.

Tamara waved a paper flag. "We know so."

Johnny scratched his head. "What's that quote by President Franklin Roosevelt on Mrs. Bingsley's desk?" It took him a minute to remember. "The only thing we have to fear is fear itself."

I sucked in my breath.

Franklin Roosevelt obviously had never met Miss Priss-A-Poo.

❀ CHAPTER 3 ❀

The Red, White, and Blue (and Green!) Crew

We started planning for the election right away. "As your campaign manager, I think we should brainstorm platform ideas."

This is what I thought he'd say:

"I still got nothing."

But this is what he really said:

"I have part of it. It's great!"

"Spill it," said Johnny. "What are you going to do for our school?"

"Thanks to my chores, an idea popped into my head." Crockett put his hand on his heart and announced, "I'm going to make our school *Green*."

Tamara looked as confused as a lost kindergartner on the first day of school. "What's wrong with the color it is now?"

I agreed. "I like the color, but a purplicious door would be fun." I whipped out a notebook that said *Top Secret*. "As your campaign manager, I don't think kids care about the color of Liberty Corner School."

Matthew asked, "Does it mean we'd have to wear green clothes and eat nothing but green veggies for lunch?"

"Shh!" I said, looking around. "Don't give my mom any ideas." I didn't want her healthy recipe radar revving up again.

Crockett turned to Johnny and clasped his hands together. "Please tell me you know what I'm talking about."

Johnny saluted Crockett. "As a fellow Junior Ranger, of course I do."

"As your campaign manager," I said, "don't you think you'd better fill me in?"

"Okay," said Crockett. "But you have to promise to stop saying, 'as your campaign manager' in every sentence."

"Deal."

"It's about our environment," said Crockett. "Going Green means making responsible decisions about our environment—where we live."

Johnny interrupted. "You show how much you care about our planet. Everything we do either helps or hurts Earth. Planting trees helps. Littering hurts. So, you work hard to do things that are friendly to our planet."

"Like recycling?" asked Tamara.

"That's one way but there's a lot more," said Crockett. "Carpooling, using cloth napkins instead of paper ones, turning off lights and computers when you're not using them . . . stuff like that."

"Boring with a capital B," I said. Crockett glared at me.

"But what does this have to do with school?" I sighed. "Kids won't care."

"I care," said Matthew. "My mom complains about all the flyers we get from school. They fill a whole bag on recycling days."

"Exactly," said Crockett. "We have 300 kids in our school. That's 300 bags a month. Since we go to school for ten months, that's 3,000 bags a year. That's a lot of trees."

No matter how much Mrs. Curtin tutored me in math, I'd never be able to add and multiply that fast. Crockett's a human calculator!

Matthew chuckled. "A lot of the flyers aren't even for me. Why did everyone get a Butterfly Scouts flyer today? That club's for girls only."

"The school could e-mail the flyers to our parents," said Crockett. "Think of the trees and the paper we'd save."

I glanced out the window and saw the trees Dad and I had planted. There were eight—one for each of my birthdays. I blurted out, "Did you know that scientists studied a tree in Malaysia that had grown over 35 feet in just 13 months?"

"I'm not surprised," said Crockett. "Trees rock." He flipped the notebook to a new page. "But Going Green is only one part of my platform. Mrs. Ammer said to find out what other kids in our class want, too."

"I want movie nights at school," said Matthew. "Wouldn't it be fun to camp out on the playground and watch them on a big screen?"

My heart thumpity thumped at the thought of seeing Penelope Parks's face on a ginormous screen.

Crockett scribbled Matthew's idea down in our Top Secret notebook.

Johnny shoved his hands into his pockets. "Ammer the Hammer will say no."

Crockett shrugged. "You never know unless you ask."

"Can you ask about having art supplies in the cafeteria during indoor recess days?" said Tamara. "Playing board games all the time gets boring."

"Sure," said Crockett, "I'll ask." Then his eyes lit up. "Wouldn't it be cool to have kids bring in things from home that they didn't want anymore?" He held up a broken ladle. "Instead of throwing this away, it could be recycled in an art project."

Tamara grabbed it. "It's perfect for one of my sculptures."

By the time everyone left, the Red, White, and Blue Crew was ready to Go Green.

Falling asleep that night was tricky. I kept thinking about the radio in the garage that I never turned off. I couldn't even count all the times I'd tossed magazines into the wrong bin or threw my water bottles into a trash can.

I didn't feel very Green. I felt blue.

❀ CHAPTER 4 ❀

A Cheatie Girl Snooper Pooper Spy

After breakfast the next day, I threw on my jean skirt and my red, white, and blue sweatshirt. I pulled my hair up and added red, white, and blue sparkly ribbons. After painting my nails with red, white, and blue glittery hearts, I used Mom's glimmery eyeliner to write Vote 4 Crockett on my face. I sparkled! Penelope Parks would be proud!

Crockett smirked when he saw me. "You look like an exploded firecracker."

I put my hands on my hips. "We agreed to look patriotic for the election."

"True . . . but you look over-the-top Penelope Parks style." He squinted. "The Vote 4 rocket on your face is interesting. Who's rocket?"

I peered into the mirror and saw a smudgy mess. "Okay—maybe I do look like an exploded firecracker."

I tossed him a Vote 4 Me T-shirt. "Here's a surprise I made for you."

When he unfolded it, this is what I thought he'd say:

"Wow! It shows off your artistic talent. Everyone will want one."

But this is what he really said:

"I'd rather lose the election than wear a shirt with hearts and glitter."

"It's just a teeny-tiny bit of glitter to outline the 4," I said. "And it's one small heart. No one will notice it."

"I did." He tossed the shirt back.

I changed the subject. "Here's our election notebook. All of your campaign promises are inside. When we meet with the Red, White, and Blue Crew today, we'll add slogan and poster ideas. It's top secret."

"My mom's taking me to get the poster board right now," Crockett said. "Want to walk with us?"

"Walk?" I shrieked. "It's ten blocks away!"

"Crockett wants to practice what he preaches," said Aunt Chrissy. "Why drive if you can walk?"

I thought of the radio in the garage and grabbed my jacket.

"That's the spirit," said Aunt Chrissy.

When we got to the store, I scooped up every poster board on the shelf. "We'll need a lot of slogans."

As we headed away from the cashier, we heard a voice. A boomy, bouncy, know-it-all voice.

"Hi, guys!" It was Miss Priss-A-Poo. "I'm so excited about the election!"

"It should be fun," said Crockett.

"What's your platform?" asked Miss Priss-A-Poo.

This is what I thought he'd say:

"My wise campaign manager advised me not to share our brilliant ideas until Monday."

But this is what he really said:

"I want to make the school . . ."

"Crockett!" I shouted before he blabbed our secrets to the entire universe. "What if she's a Cheatie Girl and steals our ideas?"

Miss Priss-A-Poo puffed her cheeks. "I wouldn't steal your ideas. I have my own. She clenched her fists and stomped. "I'm not a Cheatie Girl!"

Crockett hesitated. "Maybe we should wait until Monday." Then he changed the subject. "What are you doing here?"

"Buying poster board," she huffed.

I shoved the poster board behind my back. "There isn't any left. Sorry."

Miss Priss-A-Poo bit her lip.

"Try Shop Mart," said Crockett.

"My mom doesn't have time to take me. She's going to a wedding later so I have to get them now. What am I going to do?"

Crockett wrestled some of the poster boards from my hand. "I have ten. Take half."

Miss Priss-A-Poo jumped up and down. "That's so nice of you, Crockett. Thanks."

I leaned in to Crockett and whispered, "As your campaign manager . . ."

He cut me off. "It's only fair."

I gave him my grumpy, grumpy eyes.

By the time we got home, the rest of the Red, White, and Blue Crew were there.

"Why are there elephants and donkeys on the top of this paper?" asked Matthew when I handed out the agendas.

As campaign manager, I was ready for that question. "My dad told me that every candidate has a symbol that represents them," I said. "In the United States, there's one group of people who use an elephant and a group who use a donkey. Crockett should have an animal, too."

"How about a poodle?" said Tamara.

"Too fluffy for a boy," said Crockett. Then he shouted, "Hercules!" He grabbed a picture to show everyone. "He's my lizard that died. He's buried in the backyard."

"That was easy," I said. "Now we need slogans for posters. Something catchy."

"How about Vote for Crockett. He's the best. Better than all the rest," said Johnny.

"Not bad," said Crockett.

Matthew's eyes lit up. "How about: Crockett's like a socket. He'll electrify you!"

"Fab-u-lo-so!" I shouted.

We spent the next hour painting electrical sockets and lizards on posters. Tamara was in charge of writing the words, and I sketched the pictures. Matthew, Johnny, and Crockett painted everything.

"Those look great," said Mom. "I covered the dining room table with newspaper. Lay your posters on it to dry." Then she held up a menu. "Hungry?"

Thirty minutes later, the smell of pepperoni pizza filled the air. While we ate, Mom plopped Jack on the floor. "Can you watch Jack for ten minutes while we help Aunt Chrissy hang curtains?"

"Sure," I said.

I scooch-a-rooed onto the floor. "Watch this, everyone. Jack can pull himself up on the chair. My mom said he'll be walking soon."

Everyone waited for Jack's trick. "No," he said as he creep-a-crawled under the table.

"Fine," I said. "Be shy." I jumped back into my chair and grabbed another slice of pizza.

A minute later, we heard a shriek from the other room

I zip-a-zoomed into the dining room and couldn't believe my eyes! Miss Priss-A-Poo was covered in red, white, and blue paint and had our posters in her hands.

What was Vanessa doing sneaking around my house?

Miss Priss-A-Poo wasn't just a Cheatie Girl.

She was a spy!

❀ 𝐂𝐇𝐀𝐏𝐓𝐄𝐑 𝟓 ❀

A Star-Spangled Mess

"Why are you snooping?" asked Johnny.

"I wasn't snooping!" said Vanessa. "Honest!" She twirly whirled her hair around her finger.

I peeled posters off of the floor and swiped them out of her hands. They were smudgy and smeary. "They're ruined!"

Mom poked her head into the room. "What's wrong?" She gasped when she saw Vanessa's paint-splattered clothes. "Oh, honey, what happened?"

Before Vanessa answered, Mom's eyes bulged. She pointed to the painty streaks on the carpet. Her voice thundered, "Where's Jack?"

She followed the trail of paint to the coffee table in the living room. She bent down and pulled Jack out from underneath.

He was a red, white, and blue gooey mess.

Vanessa wiped her hands on her jeans. "I was about to ring your doorbell when I saw Jack crawling on the posters. Before I could get to him, he crawled under the table. That's when everyone came in."

Mom held Jack out in front of her like he had a stink-o, disgust-o diaper. "He must have pulled himself up on the chair and then pulled the tablecloth off of the table, posters and all."

"He's Superbaby!" said Matthew.

"A super *dirty* baby," said Mom. "You need a bath, buddy."

"No," said Jack.

"Oh yes, you do." She turned toward Vanessa. "Looks like you saved the day. Lucky for us, he only crawled about ten feet." She scrunched her eyes at me. "It was irresponsible of you to take your eyes off of him."

Irresponsible? My stomach did a flip-flop belly drop. I knew I'd have a better chance of becoming a math whiz than I would getting nominated for president now!

Aunt Chrissy came upstairs and saw the mess. "How about I scrub the carpet while you clean up your lunch dishes, Katharine?"

I grabbed our top secret election notebook and hissed at Vanessa. "I still think you were spying."

Miss Priss-A-Poo stuck her tongue out at me and grabbed a bag next to the door.

"My grandfather took me to Shop Mart. He's in the car." She handed the bag to Crockett. "I brought back your poster board."

Vanessa pointed to the pizza boxes. "Are you having a party?"

"We're the Red, White, and Blue Crew," said Matthew. "We're helping Crockett with the election."

Vanessa dug her heel into the rug. "Rebecca's away today. I'm drawing my posters by myself."

"Want us to help?" asked Tamara. "We have paint and markers."

Crockett nodded. "We can make them together." He turned toward me. "We don't have to share platforms but we can share art supplies."

Vanessa rushed outside to get permission.

"Crockett," I whispered, "it's my house and I think . . ."

"It's *our* house," said Crockett. Then he lowered his eyes. "Right?"

I zipped my lips and nodded. "Did you know that women weren't allowed to vote in an election until 1920?" With that, I skedaddled into the kitchen to clean up and tossed the pizza boxes in the recycling bin.

"This certainly is a friendly election," said Dad as he carried Jack down from his bath. "Mrs. Bingsley would be proud to know how well both candidates worked together."

Jack was squeaky-clean again. I gave him a quick kiss and whispered. "I still think Vanessa's a spy. Don't you?"

"No," said Jack.

Not even the promise of applesauce or a Bertie the Clown DVD could get him to say yes.

The Red, White, and Blue Crew— and Vanessa—spent the next three hours making more posters.

Drawing Hercules was frustrating. "I can't draw a lizard," I said erasing the poster for the fifth time.

"Me either," said Tamara. "They looked okay on the other posters."

Vanessa picked up Crockett's picture of Hercules. "Can I try?" Two minutes later, she sketched a perfect copy!

"Wow!" said Crockett. "Katharine's always said you're one of the best artists in the school."

Vanessa looked surprised. "Thanks!"

Crockett was a blabbermouth. I tossed my pencil into a cup. "I'm ready for a break."

"Me, too," said Johnny. "My hand hurts."

"How about we watch a movie?" I asked. "I'll make popcorn."

"Or," said Crockett, "we could visit Hotel Wormella."

Johnny rubbed his hands together. "That gets my vote. Wormella rocks."

Wormella was gross-a-rella. It was a worm composting bin that Crockett had built with my dad. Anytime we had fruit scraps, coffee grounds, or eggshells, we'd save them in a bucket by the sink. Then Crockett would dump them into Wormella. In a few days, the worms presto changed the trash into soil.

Everyone headed toward the door. "Aren't you coming?" asked Crockett.

Did he suddenly forget my fear of all critters big, small, and wiggly?

"Nope. I have campaign stuff to do."

"Like what?" asked Crockett.

"Like numbers five and six on the agenda." I searched for our Top Secret notebook. "Have you seen the notebook?"

"It's around here somewhere," said Crockett as he ran outside.

As I watched them from the kitchen window, Aunt Chrissy put her hand on my shoulder.

"Looks like Vanessa's interested in Crockett's worm hotel. Maybe she'll start one of her own."

"She better not start one at school," I said. "It's part of his platform."

She patted me on the back. "I'm proud of you and Crockett for having Vanessa over today."

Did I have a choice? I thought.

"No matter who wins," said Aunt Chrissy, "by working together, you'll have a great year. It reminds me of that motto: United We Stand, Divided We Fall."

If Crockett fell flat on his face and lost the election, I didn't think Vanessa would mind.

Nope. She wouldn't mind one itty-bitty bit.

❀ **CHAPTER 6** ❀

Going Green with Envy!

"I still think Vanessa's a snooper and swiped our notebook," I said at breakfast on Monday. "I can't find it anywhere."

Crockett shoved a spoonful of cereal into his mouth. "She wasn't snooping. Besides, she didn't mention Going Green for her platform."

I folded my arms. "Just because she didn't have a Green platform on Saturday doesn't mean she won't have one today."

Crockett pushed the cereal box in front of his bowl.

I pushed it back. "Sign these," I said as I slid a stack of his school pictures toward him. "I made buttons, too."

Crockett squirmed. "No one will want to wear one."

"I do," said Aunt Chrissy as she pinned it to her robe. "I'm your #1 fan."

"I want one too," said Mom. "If Vanessa has one, I'll also wear hers."

I rolled my eyes. "But you're Crockett's aunt! Not Vanessa's."

Mom picked up her apron. "Since I work at your school, I can't wear one candidate's and not the other's. It wouldn't be . . ."

"Fair and square?" I sighed.

By the time we got to school, Vanessa had already plastered her V for Victory buttons on everyone's shirts. Even Tamara, Matthew, and Johnny wore one.

The Red, White, and Blue Crew were traitors!

"Want one?" asked Vanessa.

Crockett swiped it out of her hand. "Sure."

"No thanks," I said. "Want one of Crockett's?" I tossed it to her.

She read the inscription. "Crockett's like a socket. He'll electrify you." She leaned over and snatched a marker off her desk.

Was she drawing a mustache on him? Giving him a pirate patch? "Don't doodle on it!"

Vanessa handed it back. "I drew Hercules for you."

"Thanks," said Crockett. They both walked up to Mrs. Bingsley and handed in their platforms.

A few minutes later, Vanessa shared hers with the class. "I want to have more weekend events. Wouldn't movie nights be fun? We could have sleepovers in the library and bingo nights."

She glanced at Lily. "Why wait until the end of the year for Fun Day? Maybe we could kick off the year with one and call it the Halloween Howl."

Lily clapped. "That's the best idea I've heard so far."

Vanessa continued. "Let's have Move Up Day before summer vacation. We'll get to spend one day with next year's teacher to get to know him or her."

My mouth dropped open. Those were our ideas! Every single one! Vanessa was a Cheatie Girl!

This was the perfect time to tell Mrs. Bingsley about Miss Snoop-A-Poop's Cheatie Girl ways.

"Those were Crockett's ideas," I blurted out.

Crockett took a deep breath. "Mrs. Bingsley told us to ask the class for ideas. It makes sense that some are the same."

"That explains it, Katharine," said Mrs. Bingsley. "Doesn't it?"

This is what I wanted to say:

"Vanessa is a spy. She stole our super-duper ideas."

But this is what I really said:

"Yep." My face felt like it was on fire.

Finally, it was Crockett's turn. He walked up to the board carrying the globe. "You've already heard some of my ideas, since they're the same as Vanessa's. But I have others."

He spun the globe. "This is our planet. Earth needs help, and I think I know how we can all pitch in." He opened a Band-Aid and slapped it on the United States. "I want to make our school earth-friendly. It's called Going Green."

The Red, White, and Blue Crew clapped and waved paper flags.

Then Crockett explained how our school could become Greener. "We can recycle more than just paper and water bottles. Let's compost and reduce trash in the cafeteria, too."

"Tell them about Hotel Wormella," said Vanessa.

Crockett drew pictures on the board. "My Aunt Carol uses worms to compost at home. Even if I lose, she promised to start composting here. We'll take turns dumping the bucket into the bins."

If I didn't go near the worms at home, I wasn't about to start here!

"We can plant gardens and trees," Crockett continued. "The school could use e-mail to send newsletters and notes instead of wasting paper. Let's start using both sides of our papers. These things would save a lot of trees."

He pointed to the computers near Mrs. Bingsley's desk. "We could work harder to remember to turn off lights and computers when we're not using them."

But Crockett had saved the best for last. "We have a huge wooded area behind our school. My uncle said it's about 50 acres. Wouldn't it be fun to make a nature trail and build an outdoor classroom? We just need to make some benches and tables."

Mrs. Bingsley jumped up. "My niece's school has an outdoor classroom. She's learned so much about nature. She loves it!"

Over the next few days, Crockett and Vanessa talked nonstop about the election.

At lunch, they sat at a different table to talk about the election instead of eating with us. During gym, when everyone picked partners for scooter races, Crockett chose Vanessa even though he knew I had never lost a race. When Vanessa couldn't find a book in the library, Crockett volunteered to help her find it.

But things got out of control on Thursday afternoon. When we lined up to go home, Crockett cut in front of me. "Don't forget, Vanessa. My mom will drop me off at four o'clock."

Vanessa smiled. "My dad will have the wood by then."

Now they were hanging out together like BFFs!

Then Vanessa whispered in Crockett's ear loud enough for me to hear, "My mom said you can come out to dinner with us. We're going to Wing Li's."

My stomach growled. Wing Li's was my favorite restaurant.

Before I left the classroom, I flicked off the lights and shut down the computers.

I was feeling Green alright.

Green with envy.

❊ CHAPTER 7 ❊

A Special Delivery

By the time Crockett got home from Miss Priss-A-Poo's house, I had finished my homework and was doodling *Crockett for President* on a napkin. I was bored, bored, bored.

When I saw Crockett, I barked, "When did you and Vanessa become best friends?"

"We're not best friends. I helped her dad build a Hotel Wormella."

I scrunched my eyes. "It's seven thirty! What took you so long?"

Aunt Chrissy tossed her car keys on the counter. "Mrs. Garfinkle invited us to eat at Wing Li's. It was crowded."

My eyes watered. "Did you know that almost 3 billion fortune cookies are made in the United States every year?"

Crockett ignored my interesting fact. How rude!

I pushed my chair out and stood. "Don't you want to win?"

"I wouldn't run if I didn't. But if Vanessa wins, that'll be okay, too. She has good ideas."

"But you have better ones," I said as Dad came in carrying Jack.

I waved a flag in front of Jack. "My Dad taught me about polling people to predict the winner in an election. You ask people who they're planning to vote for. So that's what I did."

Crockett looked confused. "When?"

"While you stuffed your face with Vanessa," I said. "I called everyone in the class." I waved the notebook page in the air. "Look."

"It's 10–9," I said. "Congratulations, Mr. President. You're going to cream Miss Priss-A-Poo."

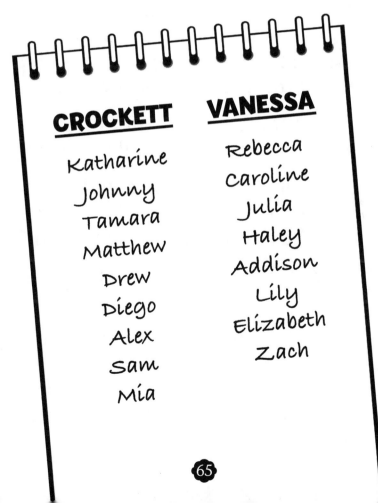

CROCKETT

Katharine
Johnny
Tamara
Matthew
Drew
Diego
Alex
Sam
Mia

VANESSA

Rebecca
Caroline
Julia
Haley
Addison
Lily
Elizabeth
Zach

"One vote isn't creaming her," said Crockett. He studied the list. "Kids could change their minds."

I smoothed the list out on the table. "You have the Red, White, and Blue Crew's vote." I ran my finger down the list. "Drew and Diego are voting for you because they copy whatever Matthew does. Alex loves your platform, and Sam and Mia are still nutty-nuts that Vanessa won the recipe contest."

"Don't take any vote for granted," said Dad. "It's not over until it's over."

Crockett agreed. "I'm still thinking of projects for the school year." His eyes lit up. "I have another recycling idea."

I chewed on my pencil eraser. "What is it?"

"It's a swap meet to trade Halloween costumes." He tilted his head. "Kids bring in their costumes from last year and get to swap for a new one."

He pointed to our Halloween picture hanging behind the kitchen table. "Unless you plan on wearing your Pirate Queen outfit from last year."

"You know I'm going to be Penelope Parks this year." I had wanted to be Penelope last year, but Rebecca bought the last costume. "Rebecca might not want to trade her costume."

"Half our school was Penelope," said Crockett. "Someone will swap with you."

I saluted him. "You're going to win easy breezy with all of your ideas." I jumped out of my chair and grabbed a package off of the counter. "I almost forgot. This came in the mail for you."

Crockett looked at the return address and shouted, "It's from my dad!" He tore open the box. "It's his lucky American flag tie!" He draped it around his neck. "It's perfect for the election."

"Perfectly patriotic!" I said.

Crockett looked at his reflection on the microwave door. "How did he know?"

Aunt Chrissy tapped her chin. "A little birdie told him you were running for president."

I knew that little birdie was Aunt Chrissy. Even though she and Uncle Greg were divorced, they had a phone meeting every Sunday night to talk about Crockett.

Crockett turned the package upside down. A letter fluttered to the floor. He scooped it up, folded it, and shoved it into his pocket. He always read his dad's letters in private.

Crockett knelt next to the recycling bins. "I'll start my homework right after the recycling is done."

After sorting through the stacks of newspapers and magazines, he noticed last week's pizza box. "This can't be recycled if it's full of grease!"

When Crockett opened the lid, we both gasped. Our Top Secret election notebook was there!

"Oops!" I slapped my head. "When I cleaned up after lunch last week, I grabbed the book off of the coffee table. I didn't want Vanessa to sneak a peek. I must have put it in the box by mistake."

"So," said Crockett, "Vanessa wasn't spying. She's *not* a Cheatie Girl."

I hug-a-rooed the book. "Guess not."

"You owe her an apology," said Crockett.

Dad nodded. Aunt Chrissy smirked.

"I don't want to apologize," I screeched. "Besides, she probably would have had a looksie, don't you think?"

Jack crawled over to me. "Jack agrees with me."

Jack blew raspberries. That's when I got an idea. "If Magic Eight Ball boy says I don't have to apologize, then I won't. Okey dokey?"

Dad nudged Aunt Chrissy and gave her a funny look.

I plunked Jack onto my lap and looked him in the eye. "Do I have to apologize to Vanessa?"

This is what I thought he'd say:

"No." Just like always.

But this is what he really said:

"Yeth." Then he squealed and banged his bottle on my head. Three times!

"There you have it," said Dad as I rubbed my head. "You'll have to apologize."

It wasn't fair!

Vanessa caused all of the explode-a-rama election drama and Jack gave me a humongous headache.

So why was I the one apologizing?

❀ CHAPTER 8 ❀

Fair and Square . . . Finally!

"**H**ow do I look?" asked Crockett. It was Election Day.

He was dressed in a blue blazer, a white shirt, tan pants, and his American flag tie. He sure didn't look like the King of the Wild Frontier. "You look like the king of the classroom."

He tugged on his tie. "I'm nervous."

"But according to my poll, you're going to win, win, win," I said. "Would the Red, White, and Blue Crew let you down?"

And if we did, Aunt Chrissy had planned a small party to pick him up.

Mom plunked a stack of pancakes on the table. "This is a special day, so I've made a special breakfast just for you: strawberry and blueberry pancakes with whipped cream."

As I watched Crockett shove-a-roo the last pancake into his mouth, I knew nothing could stop him!

Until we got to school. "Where's Diego?"

Crockett shrugged. "Maybe he's sick."

I clutched my chest. "We're doomed, Crockett. Doomed! You need his vote to win."

I zip-a-zoomed up to Mrs. Bingsley. "Diego was going to vote for Crockett. Can I vote for him?"

She took out her attendance book. "You can never be 100 percent certain who someone will vote for when there's a secret ballot." She put an X by his name. "Sorry."

I stomped back to my seat.

"Don't worry," said Crockett. "If it's a tie, Vanessa and I will be copresidents."

I whipped out the Top Secret notebook. Now that I had stapled and glued in our notes from the week, it was four inches thick. I flipped through the pages and found the polling list. Maybe I could convince Zach to vote for Crockett. Before I had a chance, Miss Priss-A-Poo skipped over.

"You found the notebook?" She jumped up and down. "Where was it?"

I covered the list. "We found it in a pizza box last night. Sorry."

Vanessa giggled. "A pizza box?" She jumped again. "I'm just glad you found it," she said as she skipped back to her seat.

My hands zapped the notebook shut. What good would it do us now?

"Is everyone ready?" asked Mrs. Bingsley as she passed out the ballots. "If so, let's vote." She looked at Crockett and Vanessa. "Good luck."

One by one, we trudged up to the ballot box and dropped our papers inside.

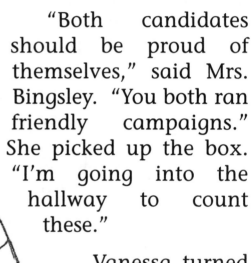

"Both candidates should be proud of themselves," said Mrs. Bingsley. "You both ran friendly campaigns." She picked up the box. "I'm going into the hallway to count these."

Vanessa turned to Crockett. "You'll make a great president."

Crockett wiped his forehead with his tie. "So will you."

I wondered if Vanessa knew that she was about to become copresident.

Mrs. Bingsley walked back in the room. "Congratulations to . . ."

This is what I thought she'd say:

"Crockett and Vanessa. It's a tie!"

But this is what she really said:

"Crockett! Let's give our new president a round of applause."

Everyone clapped as Johnny and Matthew lifted Crockett into the air.

I studied my chart and recounted the votes. Without Diego, it should have been nine to nine. Maybe Mrs. Bingsley could use a little help from Mrs. Curtin, too!

Vanessa walked over to congratulate Crockett. My stomach did a flip-flop belly drop because I knew the truth. It was a tie. Crockett should be congratulating her, too. I did not want to be a Cheatie Girl.

I tiptoed over to Mrs. Bingsley. "Are you sure you counted right? Wasn't it a tie? Nine to nine."

"I counted correctly," said Mrs. Bingsley. "Want to see?" She lifted the lid off of the box and recounted. There were ten votes for Crockett and only eight for Vanessa.

Crockett did win! I scratched my head.

"Don't look so surprised." I turned around to see Vanessa peeking over my shoulder.

"Someone lied," I said. "Someone said they were voting for you but they voted for Crockett." I scanned the classroom. "There's a Cheatie Kid around here."

Vanessa rolled her eyes. "You didn't ask everyone who they were voting for."

I scanned the list one more time. "Except for you and Crockett." I raised my eyebrows. "Did you vote for Crockett?"

She nodded. "Yep. His platform was way better than mine. He'll make a better president."

Mrs. Bingsley overheard. "Katharine, I'm proud of you. When you thought I goofed, you did the honest and fair thing."

My heart pounded. "Are you saying that I acted fair and square?"

She smiled. "That's what I'm saying. Lady Liberty's going to be proud of you when I tell her."

I jumped up and down. "Watch out Vanessa. Now that I really am a fair and square kind of girl, someone might nominate me for president next year!"

Vanessa put her arm around my shoulder. "Maybe I will. If . . ."

"If what?" I asked.

"If you promise not to lose your election notebook in a pizza box again."

We laughed and walked over to the group huddled around Crockett. He was talking about the Halloween Costume Swap.

He gave me the V for Victory sign. "I want to thank Katharine for being the best campaign manager ever!"

Everyone clapped. Even Vanessa.

I felt sparkly. Shiny. Shimmery.

It was definitely going to be a star-spangled year.